My *Twisted* LIFE

Damian Wilson

NEWMAN SPRINGS PUBLISHING
320 Broad Street
Red Bank, NJ 07701

First originally published by Newman Springs Publishing 2024

ISBN 979-8-89061-535-0 (Paperback)
ISBN 979-8-89061-536-7 (Digital)

Printed in the United States of America

Chapter 1

Alice is in the kitchen cooking, preparing a meal for her husband James, and she hears the front door opening. "Honey, I'm in the kitchen getting the food ready. Go take a shower and get ready." Alice nervously listens to see if James is walking to their room out of fear that he's having a bad day and will come take it out on her. It wouldn't be the first time he beat her and then beg for forgiveness.

"Hey, honey, the food is ready. Sit down and have some. What do you want to drink? I'll get it for you."

"Fuck! You can't get shit right, even something as simple as this."

Alice shakes as if her life came to an end and doesn't know what will happen next. "It tastes all right to me. Is there something you don't like?" Alice is stuttering. "I can whip you up something else if it's not to your taste."

James throws the plate off the table and yells, "Fucking hoe, this not what I asked for! Where the fuck your head be? You had one job, and you fuck that up."

"Look at yourself, you said you would change. James, I can't keep doing this."

James rushes over with his hands clasped together. "Baby, baby, I'm sorry. I didn't mean to scare you." James is kissing on her and trying to get her to forgive him, but Alice has seen enough, so she pushes him off her. "I'm about to go take a shower and go to sleep. You can clean up everything."

Later, James is sitting in the living half-drunk and decides to go up to the room. "Baby, wake up. Give me some of that pussy."

Alice says softly, "No, James, I'm not in the mood from what you pulled downstairs."

James starts to rub on her and kisses on her neck.

"Stop! James, I'm not in the mood. Why can't you change?"

James grabs her arm and kisses her as he puts the other hand in her golden place.

"No, can you please stop?"

James grabs her neck and puts his already erect penis inside her. James talks and thrusts at the same time, faster and faster. "I can fuck my own wife, can't I? If you would have let me do what I wanted to do, we could have saved time."

Alice lies there crying. "How could you? How could you?" She turns her head away, not wanting to see the monster on top of her enjoying himself.

*****

Alice walks to the mailbox with her hair blowing in the wind and her sundress dancing with every breath taking step.

"Hey there, Miss Alice. You're looking beautiful as always."

"Oh, hey, Beth. I think you're doing better than me. Look how your butt looks in them pants."

"Oh, stop it. The wind picked up a little out here, but hey, do you think you can peek in on Tyler when you have time? You know how teens can be nowadays."

"Oh yes. I don't have my own yet, but I know. I'll make sure he doesn't burn the house down."

"Did you hear that, Tyler? Don't mess my house up."

Tyler stands at the door and sees Alice; he can't help but to think of all the things he would do to a lady as beautiful as her. "Hey, Miss Alice. Bye, Mom. You acting like this some new."

A few hours later, Alice walks over to her neighbor Beth's house to see what Tyler is doing and uses a spare key Beth gave her. As she walks through the door and comes in, she sees Tyler at the fridge in his underwear with his pure white body and blond hair with a print. She can't help to stare at it and blushes from it till she looks him in his blue eye that draws her in.

"Oh, I'm sorry. I didn't hear you come in. Let me go put some clothes on."

"Okay, it's big."

"What you say, Miss Alice? I didn't hear you."

Alice covers up her mouth. "Oh nothing, just thinking about some big shit. No, I'm picking up something."

"Here I come. Do you need any help with anything at your house? My mom told me to help you if you need some help."

"Oh, no, I'm fine for now. You just keep some pants on. I got to go."

Alice goes to a medical store and buys extra-strong sleeping pills, then has a flashback of her mother being heavy addicted to pills and other drugs. She asks herself, *How did I end up in another fucked-up situation like this?*

The next morning, Alice's husband's parents call and ask them out to eat. "My baby, why you never come and visit your momma?"

"You know I be busy, Momma, but I got a little time. I'm gonna stop by today."

"Okay, baby, I'll let your father know."

"Okay, Ma, I'll see you later." He then turns to his wife. "Alice, throw some on. We going to my mom's house, and you better not embarrass me."

At James's parents' house, they sit around the table, and Alice is praying they don't set him off.

"James, how have things been."

"Stressed, Mom, at work, trying to get a raise."

"Oh, I'm so proud of you. I knew you were gonna be a hard worker."

"All right, let's not brag on the boy too much. We know he has his mistakes and problems."

"Oh, you hush! You are always trying to bring him down."

"Mom, it's all right."

"Yeah, I know it's all right because you know what you do and don't do."

James's dad is saying something under his breath. "Look how nervous that girl looks, you know he ain't right."

"What you say, Bill?"

"I said I bet he is not getting any help with that temper of his."

"Well, he ain't go off on you yet, so he must be doing some right."

"The day he goes off on me will be the day I send him back to the good Lord, God forgive me."

"Shut up, Bill. Alice, baby, how he's been treating you?"

Alice nervously thinks of something to say and is trying not to let them see her panic. "Everything been good. With James working a lot, we try to find time for each other. We making it work. Hopefully his work will stable out soon."

"James, now you make sure you spend some time with her and treat her right."

"He need to do more than that." *Poor girl* are Bill inner thoughts. *Poor girl. I pray he not treating her too bad.*

James and the family continue to talk. Alice is feeling happy for the warmth she gets from James's parents and asks herself how they can be so different.

James and Alice leave and get in the car. Before they can even leave, he reaches over and hits her in the lip with the back of his hand. "Bitch, you made me do it. You gonna sit up and make it look like I'm not putting no work into this marriage. You couldn't just say some to make me look good. You had to throw some shade."

"I just ain't know what to say! You just don't care how you act anymore."

"Look, I'm sorry. You know I have a lot on my plate, and I need you to have my back. I can't do this alone."

"You can't do it alone?" Alice laughs. "And I'm getting tired of this." Alice turns her head toward the window and thinks about all the stuff she put up with and asks herself, *How can I get out this hell that keeps pulling me in deeper and deeper into despair?*

Alice and James make it home. Alice lies down on the bed next to James's phone when he suddenly gets a text. "Hey, baby, what time you coming by tonight? I can't wait to get some more off you. I know your wife can't please you like I do, so let me know you on the way so I can get ready."

"James! *James!*" Before Alice screams again, she stops out of fear for what James would do to her because of his unstable behavior.

"Babe, I'm going out with the boys. It's gonna be real late, so I'm just gonna stay over one of the house."

"Okay," Alice says as she lies down crying with a confused feeling. *How can I cry for such a person? How can I love such a person? Why must I bear so much pain for such a person?* Alice can't help but to break down again.

Ding dong!

Alice goes to the door where she welcomes Tyler. "Hey, Tyler, do you need anything?"

"My mom sent me over to see if you had any wine for family night. But, Miss Alice, it looks like you crying. What's wrong? I can get my mom for you if you—"

Before Tyler can finish his sentence, Alice falls in his arms. Tyler grabs Alice with a face of concern and worry. Alice hugs Tyler and feels his embrace and a warmth that she hasn't felt in a while.

"Tyler, what took you so long?"

"I was helping Miss Alice move something. Her husband's not there right now."

"Well, if she need help and you around, help her out since she always help us."

"Okay, I will."

Alice is standing in a daydream with her arms wrapped around herself. She sits down on the couch confused with a happy yet lustful face. *How can I get this feeling from a teenager? What was my mind thinking? Calm down, calm down.*

Out of nowhere, she gets a text from an unknown number. Text Unknown. Alice looks at the text and sees a picture of James lying down with another woman's hands on his chest.

Alice's face shows a look of disgust and disappointment. Another text comes to her phone. "This pain that you feeling is only the beginning. I will make you feel much more."

Alice sits there and thinks, *What have I done to deserve such things? Why am I being tortured?*

The next morning, Alice gets a call from Beth. "Hey, me and the family are going out to eat since we haven't been spending a lot of time eating out really. I was wondering if you and James wanted to go."

As soon as she hears James's name, anger boils up to the point where she has to calm down and fix her face that has a terrible expression. "Well, I would have to ask that ass— Oh, I'm sorry, ask James because he been busy lately with his job."

"Okay, well, just get back to me. We leaving around six o'clock."

Alice looks up because she hears James coming in the house. "Hey, Beth, hold on. He just walked in."

"Who you on the phone with?"

"It's Beth. She asked if we wanted to go out with them to eat. It would be nice to go out since we haven't done anything like that in a while."

"One second, let me check my schedule."

"What, your cheating schedule?"

"Did you say anything?"

"Oh no, nothing at all."

"Well, I'm free, so yeah."

James and Alice head out to meet Tyler and his mom at the restaurant. While in the car driving, James keeps looking at his phone, and Alice looks at him nervously. She knows he is having an affair.

Someone pulls up to James and Alice's house with a hat to cover up their face and a black jacket. The stranger takes out a pick set and breaks into house. The stranger walks around house, looking at the pictures on the wall and other things. "I see you been living a good life off others' sacrifice, not caring about nobody but yourself. Let's shake this happy home up some more and see how you like it then."

The stranger walks to James and Alice's room, takes a condom out, and puts something in it to make it look used.

At the restaurant, James is still looking at his phone and texting. Alice looks at him with pain and agony. "I have to go to the bathroom."

Tyler notices something is wrong with her and says he's gotta use the bathroom too. "Miss Alice, you in there?" Tyler opens the door and sees her crying. "Miss Alice, why you crying?"

"Because James is having an affair."

"Why haven't you said anything or leave him?"

"He will beat me if I say some about it."

Tyler hugs and kisses Alice. Alice is in shock and disbelief. "Tyler, why did you kiss me?"

"I'm sorry, I don't know what came over me. That hug from last time and everything else got me confused. Please don't tell my parents."

"I'm not, but don't let it happen again."

Tyler and Alice walk back to the table and continue to eat.

"Alice, you and James never thought about having a child?"

"Well, I have, and we been trying, but it never happened, so we went to the doctor, and it turns out James's count is low, so we have to try other options."

James sits there looking embarrassed, shows a fake smile, and says, "Hey, we gone get one" as he hugs Alice.

Soon, James and Alice are getting in the car, getting ready to leave.

"Why would you do that?"

"Do what, James?"

"You told them I couldn't have kids. Do you know how embarrassed I felt? If it's a big problem for you, then go have some stranger's baby and raise it by yourself!" he tells Alice with an irritated face expression.

"I didn't mean to, James." Alice looks out the window once again and thinks about her lost baby.

James and Alice pull up to their house.

"James, we need to have a talk."

"What we need to talk about?"

"I will tell you when we get in the house."

James and Alice enter the house. Alice is thinking if this is the right decision.

"So what we need to talk about?"

"I know you been having an affair."

"What the fuck you talking about!"

"You know exactly what I'm talking about, James. I saw the messages."

"So you going through my phone now? Where the trust at?"

"No, you were in the shower, and she texted your phone. Who is she, James?"

"She a nobody, just someone I work with."

"How could you do me like this?"

"I'm not in love with you anymore, what can I say."

"What do you mean you don't love me anymore, James?"

"I just don't, Alice. I think we should get a divorce. I feel like you're not good for my health and growth."

The stranger in black is hiding near the house, trying to listen and see if they find her surprise she left.

"I'm a good wife to you. I have food and your bathwater ready for you when you get home from work. I sacrifice so much for you, James. How could you do me like this? And all I do is show you love, even when I was attacked and raped by you."

Alice starts hitting James in the back.

James turns around and punches her. "Bitch, keep you hands off me. I do what I want to do, you have no say so."

They start fighting and throwing things and arguing again. Tyler hears them and peeps out his bedroom window.

"Get out my house, James!"

"I will leave!" James then pulls his phone out and calls someone.

The stranger's phone rings, so she answers and talks to the person on the other end.

"Baby, can you come get me?"

The stranger replies, "Yeah, babe, I'm not that far out. I'll be there." The stranger sneaks back to her car, waits ten minutes, then pulls up. The black car pulls up and blows the horn.

Tyler is still looking out the window, wondering what's going on and if he should go see after what he did.

"I'm out, but I will be talking to my lawyer about the divorce."

"Just leave, James. I have had enough. I don't need nothing from you, I'm good without you."

James walks out slamming the door and pulls off with a mysterious person.

Tyler then runs over to check on Alice. Tyler walks in the house and finds Alice on the floor crying. "What happened, Mrs. Alice?"

"I confronted him, but it was no use. I give up."

Tyler hugs on Alice and picks her up. "It's all right, he don't deserve you. You're beautiful, intelligent, smart. I love everything about you. You can do way better."

Alice looks Tyler in the eyes as she hears his words that tug at her heart. She kisses Tyler as he holds her. They start making love where they stand in the living room.

James out of nowhere comes back home to the surprise of Tyler on top of Alice on the floor.

"You fucking hoe. You fucking the neighbor's son, a fucking teenager? How low can you go?"

James rushes toward Alice and Tyler and pulls him off and starts to choke her, but then Tyler pushes him off and start wrestling with him till he twists his ankle and falls into a glass table. James gets glass stuck in different parts of his body.

The stranger who is waiting outside for James hears glass breaking and thinks of a memory where she killed her stepdad to protect a twin sister she now despises for sending her to prison for something she did to help her.

"Help me! Help! Call for help please!" James cries on the floor as blood runs out, his body full of different cuts.

"We got to call for help and help him."

Alice screams. "No! We gotta end this once and for all!" She runs over to James.

"No, please! Don't! No, I'll do anything—"

She stabs him in his neck before he can finish another empty lie.

Alice looks at the body and quickly starts to make it look like he died from the glass, even though he was already bleeding out.

The stranger runs in to see what happened because she no longer hears anything. To her surprise, James is lying surrounded by broken glass, dead. She looks up and makes eye contact with Alice and runs off.

Alice is in disbelief and stands there in shock from the person she has just seen.

The police arrive on the scene and question Tyler and Alice.

"Does he have to go to jail?"

"No, ma'am, we got a statement from them, but it seems like Tyler had more to say. I would keep an eye on him."

"Tyler, what was you doing over there?"

Tyler stutters out, "I heard a big argument going on, so when James left, I went over to help Miss Alice clean up, but then he came back and went crazy."

"Okay, baby, it's all right, baby. Let's go home."

The police officer on the scene can tell some don't add up and makes it clear that he would keep an eye out.

Days later, Alice is getting ready for the funeral Alice goes to her room to get something and finds a used condom on the floor. Alice, with a surprised and confused look, starts thinking about how it got there. Alice starts to tap on her and decides to forget about it.

At the funeral, people are whispering, "I figure she used to this since they killed they own mother and stepdad."

"No, I heard it was just the dad. Her mom was a crackhead."

Alice hears the whispers and puts her head down in pain.

"Hey, baby, you all right? I know you tried your best for him. I don't blame you. We know James had some bad ways, and they got the best of him."

"Bill, you gonna talk about him at the funeral?"

"Well, if you would have listened to me, this wouldn't have happened."

"Baby, I'm sorry."

"I'll leave you to it."

"Bill, he was you son too."

"Yeah, he was, but you raised him like he was only yours. Now look at us."

Outside the funeral, a girl in black watches with a sinister look on her face, waiting for Alice to come out. "Hey, Miss Perfect, how that pain feel? Shit got real enough for you yet?"

"You did me a favor, so try again. Oh wait, how you feeling since you was fucking him too?"

The girl looks down and walks off.

*****

A couple days later, while getting ready to go for a little walk with his family, Tyler calls Alice, telling her he can't sleep, that they need to come clean.

"Alice, I can't sleep. Every time I close my eyes, I see his face. I hear him crying for us to save him. I keep living like this, and the way he looked when you stabbed him, I can't forget the way life left his body. Why you did it? I told you I was there for you. You should've just helped him. The rest we could have figured out later."

"It's we, Tyler. We did it together, so if I go down, you going down too. If you would have stayed away from me, I wouldn't have did what I did. So I advise you to think this through and don't make any foolish mistakes."

"No! I wanted to help him, but you ran and killed him. I didn't want it to go like this! You kissed me! You was my first!"

Tyler's mom Beth hears him scream. "Tyler, you all right? If you don't wanna go, we don't have to."

Tyler covers the phone and yells back, "I'm all right, Mom, we can go."

"Okay, just making sure. We'll be waiting downstairs."

"Miss Alice, please don't make me do this alone and against you. I know you was just trying to escape, but it's not right."

"You think they gone care? You let me kill him and then didn't say a word! You think you gone get off with a slap on the wrist? This your sin too."

"No, you did what you wanted to do. How was I supposed to stop you?"

"Tyler, just go think about it. Tyler, this won't end nicely. I tried to be on your side to help you."

In a low voice, he replies, "We will see."

Alice knows she can't let that happen, so she starts thinking of a way to fix it.

Later that day, Tyler is going for a walk with his mom and dad to help him get over his bad memories from that day.

"Tyler, you got everything?"

"Yeah, he got everything. I made sure."

"Yeah, Mom. I'm 'bout to look around before we walk on the trail."

"Okay, don't go anywhere just yet. We almost ready. Did anybody pack some sunscreen?"

"Now that's something I forgot about, baby. Sorry."

Across from Tyler's family is another family getting ready.

"Look, Dad's old bow."

"Damn, Alex put that thing back in the truck before you hurt yourself."

"He ain't hurting nothing. It's good he taking a interest in something I like and do. We gone go camping soon, son, just put it back in the car, save you mom a heart attack. She don't like things like that."

"Yes, and for good reason too. They dangerous and shouldn't be played with."

Okay, Dad, I'm 'bout to."

"I said now, Alex."

Alex talks to himself. *Let me see, can I pull it back with a arrow one time?* Alex struggles to pull the string back all the way. "Oh shit! Damn!"

"What happened, Alex?"

At the other side of the parking area, Tyler screams out in pain. "Mom! Mom! Help me!"

"Honey, what's wrong?" Beth sees Tyler on the ground with an arrow in his thigh. "Ben! Ben! Come here, hurry up please!"

"I'm coming, I'm coming! What happened? How…how did this happen?" Ben grabs Tyler lightly. "Who the fuck is shooting arrows."

Alex's dad and mom rushes over. "Oh my god, I'm so sorry! Our son was playing around and shot the arrow by accident. What can we do to help?"

"Get the f—— back. How can you let him play with that in the open at a trail? How stupid can y'all be? If you would train your child right, this wouldn't happen!"

"We are so sorry, let's try to call the police."

Before they can even get done, Ben runs Tyler to the car and tells Beth to drive while he tries to stop the bleeding some type of way.

"Mom, Mom, it hurts. Dad, don't let me die. I don't wanna die."

Ben tries his best to stop the bleeding, which seems to slowed down.

Ring ring ring, ring ring ring.

Ben sees Tyler phone ringing and decides to answer it.

"Hello, can I speak to Tyler?"

"Who is this? Tyler can't talk right now."

"I'm Miss Alice. I was calling to ask Tyler if he can he help me put something together."

"He can't right now, somebody's son shot him with an arrow."

"Ah, my god, is he all right?" Alice begins to smile as she knows this can help her with her problem.

"I don't know, we going to Hales Hospital."

"Okay, I'll meet y'all there."

Beth turns her hazard lights on and speeds toward the hospital. Halfway there, there's a family walking on the sidewalk with a daughter and a dog. The daughter holds the dog, but it gets away and runs toward the street. Beth swerves out the way and misses the girl, but shakes the car badly, which causes Tyler's thigh to bleed even more.

"Dammit, what happened?"

"I'm sorry, there was a little girl in the road."

Ben looks at Tyler, who passes out from the pain. "Hold on, buddy, we're almost there."

They make it to the hospital and call for help, and a doctor comes and gets them.

"Do any of y'all have the same blood type as him?"

"No, he's adopted."

"Well, we need to find somebody with an O type fast."

"Alice, I remember you saying you have an O type. Can you do it?"

Alice at the side thinks her problem solved itself and can only say yes.

"Get her blood test, and get me the results."

The nurse who was half sleep from overworking doesn't remember what test the doctor exactly asked for because she's tired and hasn't slept much, so she tests the blood for the type, DNA, and pregnancy.

"Here you go, all the tests."

"I didn't ask for all these. I asked to only check and see do they blood match."

"I'm sorry, I'm sorry. It won't happen again."

"If you can't handle the job, leave."

"I can, it won't happen again. It shows that they're related, and she's pregnant."

"That's not our job. Don't overstep."

Left in a room alone, Tyler is barely holding on, waiting on his transfusion. Alice takes the moment to finish him off. Alice gets a pillow and puts it over Tyler's head, doing whatever it takes to keep her secret.

The doctor runs into the room and sees Tyler dead. They try their best to bring him back but can't.

"Ma'am, I couldn't save him. He was stable at first. We do not know what went wrong. We really tried to see, but I'm sorry for your loss."

"Oh no, not my baby! Not Tyler! Ben, he's gone, my baby. Tyler, he's gone! He's all we had."

"I know, baby, calm down. Try to calm down. I know it's hard. I'm here."

"I'm sorry, ma'am. There are some other things I have to tell y'all, but it can wait if y'all need time."

"No, no, you can say it here."

Alice, who is hiding around, staying out of sight, decides to run to the bathroom.

James's second lover, the girl in black, shows up in the hospital using a tracker she talks him into putting on Alice phone. The girl sees what's going on and steals one of the nurses' jackets to get closer and hear what Beth and the doctor are talking about and is surprise about what she hears.

"I know this might be a bad time to bring this up, but one of my nurses ran a DNA test, and it came back positive for relations. Is it possible for him and Mrs. Alice to be mother and son? Till we test further, we won't know."

Beth is crying and leaning on her Ben. "Tyler is not our biological son, and I thought adopting would be a good way to give back to the world, and we never got around to having another baby because he was all we needed. If this is true, then I think she should know that she's kin."

"I thought James couldn't have kids?"

Beth understands where her husband's thoughts are coming from till the doctor says, "Sometimes, cases like that happen."

The girl thinks, *How can that be?* Because she too knows James was having a problem with getting Alice pregnant, and the chances were below 20 percent. Suddenly, a light went off in her head, only she had no way to prove it.

The girl looks at her phone and sees Alice moving again and decides to get out the way and hide.

In a bathroom, Alice gets nauseous and throws up. After she cleans herself up, she starts to walk back toward Tyler's room.

As she gets the news from Beth, her mind can't help but spiral out of control, so she walks away in a state of confusion, holding her stomach, knowing the baby is likely Tyler's.

The girl looking at Alice's expression knows what that look is for and can't help but laugh at how funny the situation is to her.

Alice returns home and sits down on the living room floor where she cries, holding some plan B pills.

Next door, Ben's trying his best to console Beth and help her get through this tragedy, even though he's going through the same thing.

"Our son, our son. He's gone! They said he was stable, but now, he's gone. What we gonna do? He was all we had."

"It's all right, he's safe now. We got to pull through so he won't worry about us. Come on, let's try to go to bed. It's been a long day. You need some sleep."

Ben walks Beth to the room, then fixes her some water with a sleeping pill to help her sleep.

Meanwhile, at James's second lover's house, Alesha starts plotting something to destroy Alice's life even more on a whiteboard with notes on it.

Days later at the police station, Police Officer Jackson, who was at the scene of James's death, sits thinking about his next move.

"Ay, Jackson, did you hear about the boy that died? Wasn't he at one of your crime scenes?"

Jackson stands up as fast as he can with a serious look on his face. "Now I'm a little suspicious." Jackson plays back the scene in his head and remembers how Tyler looked, like there was more going on. Jackson asks around and figures out what hospital Tyler was at and heads that way.

Jackson asks if he can see the tapes from the camera pointed toward Tyler's room.

"I wish I can help you, but the cameras were down for maintenance in that area."

Jackson slams his hand on the table. "Dammit!"

Jackson leaves the hospital and goes toward Alice's house and sees Miss Alice coming out the house about to head to Tyler's funeral.

"I just came to check on you since two people connected to you have died. I thought you'll need somebody to talk to."

"For god sake, I'm going to my relative's funeral, and you come to my house and harass me?"

I'm not here to bother you, I'm just making sure you all right. I know you been through a lot, and as an officer, it's my job to keep tabs on certain things," he says in a sarcastic way.

"Well, I'll let you get to it." Alice gets in her car and lets out a long breath of air. *And I thought my life was gonna get better, but look at me.*

At the funeral, Tyler's casket is being lowered down, and Beth cries as she watches. Alice hugs her and gives her to Ben to be walked out.

A boy walks up to Ben and Beth. "My name is Jason. I'm a friend of Tyler. I just wanted to say sorry for your loss."

Beth hears him and gets weak in the knees. "Oh, I'm sorry, baby. I'm sorry."

"Thank you. I'm sorry we can't talk, but I have to calm her down and get her home, but it's nice to meet you."

"Okay." Jason shakes Ben's hand and leaves.

Jason puts his face down, not knowing what to do with this pain he's feeling.

Alice walks away and heads toward her car. Out of nowhere, Alesha steps out and whispers to her, "How does it feel to have your life destroyed with nobody to lean on? And I wonder how Beth would feel if she found out about the truth of you and Tyler?"

Alice's face freezes as if her heart stopped.

"Don't worry, I'm not gone tell yet. I'm gonna take my time and enjoy you torture yourself."

Outside the funeral, Jackson sits watching the scene, wondering what can cause Alice to make that face and why she has a twin sister who showed up out of nowhere. Jackson follows Alesha, who walks away, to what looks like her car and pulls up beside her. Jackson lets the window down. "Hey, can I talk to you for a second?"

"I don't know you. Why would I talk to you?"

"I'm a police officer. I just wanna ask you a couple questions."

"Sorry, but I can't right now, but if you give me your number, I'll tell you when I'm free."

"Okay, it's **********."

"Okay, be looking for a text."

Jackson drives off, and Alesha gets in her car with a thinking face on, a face of pleasure seeing Alice in pain.

Two days later, Beth is in Tyler's room cleaning up and looking through his phone. Beth sees that Tyler was texting a friend named Jason.

Tyler: wyd
Jason: nothing chilling
Jason: do you have them earrings I let you borrow
Tyler: I have one I think I lost the other one at this girl house
Jason: do you know how long I had them, them was my favorite
Jason: so did you at least hit dude, and where she from put me on
Tyler: you know it but
Jason: but what bro
Tyler: she stay nearby, she's a little older and something happened
Jason: what was it bad
Jason: ????
Tyler: yes I can't say over the phone, I'll tell you the next time I see
you
Jason: dude you really gonna do me like this
Tyler: look I'm going through a lot
Jason: I know, bro I didn't mean it like that

Beth sees that Tyler doesn't reply to last message. She calls Ben in to come and look. "Come and look at this. He was texting someone named Jason about a girl. I think something was wrong."

Ben looks at the message. "I see, baby, but he's gone now. Ain't no sense in looking into it. Don't do this to yourself. Come on, take a break and clear your head."

*****

Alesha is in her apartment thinking and working out her plan and decides to call Jackson.

"Hello?"

"Hey, I'm calling to let you know I'm free."

Jackson looks at his phone confused. "Look! I don't have time for games. Who is this, and what do you want!"

This Alesha. If I knew you was gonna treat me like this when I call, I would have just tossed your number."

Jackson drops his food that he was eating. "Oh shit. I'm sorry, I didn't think you was gonna call. You trying to meet up now?"

"Well, yeah, that is the reason you gave me this number. Come to my place later."

Alesha stands at a box with duct tape and drugs. Only the Lord himself know what she's got planned for poor Jackson. Only time will tell.

*****

Ding dong!
"Who is it?"
"It's Jason."
Beth gets happy and runs to the door like she won a prize or something. What can get her so happy?
"Hey! Jason, come in, how you doing?"
Ben is sitting at the side. *Oh lord, not again.*
"Jason, I saw some of you and Tyler's texts."
Jason gets nervous and starts to freeze up.
"Oh, baby, it's nothing bad. I'm just trying to see if you know the girl Tyler was involved with."
"No, he said he was gonna tell me all about it when we see each, but I never got the chance to meet with him."
Beth's facial expression drops. "It's all right, baby. You can go to his room. Do you know the way?"
"Yes, ma'am. I been over once."
"You happy now?"
"Do you have a problem with me taking an interest in who my son was hooking up with?"
"Did you even know he was seeing someone?"
"No, baby. I just want what's best for you and to help us get through this."
"I know I had shortcomings as a father and as a husband. It might be a little late, but I'm here now, and I'm trying to do better."
"Okay, baby. I'll stop."

*****

Later that night, Jackson is pulling up to Alesha's apartment and walks to the door number she gave him.

Knock knock knock.

Alesha opens door and lets him in and walks to the kitchen. "Have a seat!"

"I just want you to know I'm not interested in games. You know what I came here for. Don't hold me up. I know how cunning you sisters are, I can feel it."

"Well, since you put it that way, go ahead and ask away. I'll try to answer all your questions."

"Well what was it that you told Alice to get her to make such an expression?"

"What you mean?"

"Did you bring me here to play games?"

"Well, I guess I can tell you. Before that, let me get you something to drink. This a long story."

Alesha goes and gets a dark cup and pours some liquor in it. She sneaks and puts some strong medicine in it that she had for this very moment.

"Here you go, drink this."

Jackson puts the cup down on the table.

"You can at least drink it."

Jackson drinks the liquor in one go with an attitude and says, "It's gone. Now talk."

"Well, she was shocked to see me because I been away for a while, and we haven't seen each other for years. I was in town and started hearing stories of what was going on."

"Fuck, I don't wanna hear this shit. I came to—"

Before he can finish the sentence, he starts to get dizzy and unstable, barely able to talk, and falling over.

"What you put in this?"

Alesha quickly picks him up and walks through the hall, where she sees an old couple walking to their room. "Everything good, he just had a little too much to drink."

Alesha puts him in the car and starts driving, but to where?

Going down a road with woods, Alesha pulls to the side and opens the trunk. There's a man taped up. Alesha throws him out the trunk and walks to the car and gets the police gun.

The man tries to crawl away till Alesha shoots him in the head before he can make a sound. She cleans the gun and puts the police beside the body with the gun in his hand and begins taking pictures.

The police finally starts to wake up to what seems to be a nightmare, one he doesn't remember a thing about.

Oh my god, no no no! I didn't do this, I didn't do this! Jackson starts to panic. *Yes, yes, a shovel. Make it disappear, make it disappear. Nobody seen me, nobody seen it. Dig dig dig! Lord, how can I do this, Lord? How can I do this? I didn't do it.*

Jackson finally covers the body and starts to run till he catches a ride.

*****

At Beth's house

"I'm sorry, honey. I was the one who told you to chase your dreams, that I was gonna help take care of the house and our son, but still got sidetracked on my own work. Maybe if I was home more and did things differently, this wouldn't have happened. I been trying to stay strong for the both of us, but I can't no more. I miss him too, Beth."

"I know, baby. It's all right. Come here. It's all right, you don't have to be strong for me. Let it out, baby."

Ben cries as his lies in Beth's arms, finally letting go of some of the pain he is holding on to, which comes from being the man of the house and not knowing what was going on with his own son.

The next morning, outside of Alesha's house, Jackson stands with a doubtful look. "Alesha, I know you in there. Come out! Dammit, come out!"

Before he can even knock, Alesha opens the door, heading out.

"What happened last night? I can't remember a thing. I woke up at home not knowing how I got there. This ain't happened till I met with you."

"You drank a little too much, remember? I had to stop you. I think you're worrying about too much stuff. Stress kills."

"Well, do you happened? Do you know where my car at?"

"I don't know, I had to send you away when you started getting aggressive and pulling on me. I was getting scared for my safety."

"I don't remember that. I'll never do anything like that. I have to go, something's not right."

At Tyler's grave, Beth and Ben are visiting Tyler and sees a woman in a black coat, and it turns out to be Alice.

"What you doing out here by yourself?"

Beth bumps Ben and grabs Alice's hand. "I'm sorry, Miss Alice. I know it got to be hard on you too."

"To find out you have family around and for that family to leave you so soon. For that family to be taken. He was taken, and we know if he wasn't shot, this wouldn't have happened, and I think we need to have a talk with the police and that family."

"Please stop. It was an accident. I don't want to destroy that boy's life, and I know he didn't mean to."

"You wanted to find out who he was having sex with, but don't wanna punish the kid who did this to him?" Ben points at the grave as he talks.

Alice says nervously, "Okay, okay, let's calm down. We don't wanna argue in front of Tyler and disappoint him. We got to help each other make it through this. I probably ain't get to know him like y'all did as his parents, but I think he wouldn't want y'all fighting."

"Okay, we will have this talk another time. I'll let it go for now."

"Alice, you don't need to be in this wind. You got to treat your body better for the baby."

"Okay, well, let me go and give y'all some alone time. Don't stay out too long. Beth, you do know that boy that shot Tyler gone be arrested. Either way, they have to take him in."

Beth starts crying. "No one wins." And she hugs Ben.

*****

The next day, Jackson is sitting at his desk at work and gets a text from an unknown sender. It's pictures of him and the dead body. Jackson jumps up, looking at his phone.

"Jack, you good? Did you find out who took your car yet?"

"I'm chasing down a lead."

"Do you need any help?"

"I'm good, I got it under control. You get out there and catch some criminals."

The unknown sender texts, "I know what you did, but don't worry you did a good deed that man raped young girls but had too many connections and slipped away every time be happy you took such a person out this world, but this is not the end we got more work to do."

*****

At the house of the boy who shot the arrow, the police pulls up and knocks on the door. Tasha, the mom, asks, "Who is it?"

"It's the police, open up."

Tasha's face goes pale from this moment she knew was coming. Tasha falls to the floor. "They came to take my baby away! It was a accident, it was a accident. Baby, tell them he didn't mean to do it. He didn't know what he was doing."

"Get up. We knew this was coming. You got to be strong for him and support him through this."

Knock knock knock.

"The police! Open up."

Tasha falls again as Terry tries to get her up.

"Tasha, please, get it together!"

Knock! Knock! Knock!

"This the police, open up, or we will knock this door down."

Terry drops Tasha and runs to the door. "Wait wait wait!" Terry opens the door. "Come on in, no need for that. My wife is having a hard time, please understand."

Meanwhile in his room, Alex sits in the dark corner crying. Because of this devastating mistake he made, his life can be ruined, but is that the only thing he is thinking about? Can the only thing he be thinking about is his life? Because either way, the blood is still on his hands.

"Ma'am, we held off as long as possible due to the victim's mother's plea to give y'all time to come to terms with things, but we have to bring your son in. This has to happen."

Tasha, the wife, tries her best to get it together, but the thought of her son doing time keeps knocking her to the ground.

As I look at the lives of this family from the outside, I ask myself why must they only think of themselves when such a tragic thing happened? Have any taken the time to say sorry to Tyler and not think about what they got, not think about how his death affected them? Have you thought about the person who died and how sad they feel to leave everything behind? Pain goes both ways.

Tasha is still going on about something she can't change. "It was an accident! He didn't mean it. He's still a child." Tasha grabs on the police. "You can't take him!"

The police officer on the right gently pushes her away before Terry can react. "Sir, you need to get your wife and calm her down. I'll hate to have to arrest her too."

"Sir, where's the direction to your son's room."

Terry can't help but to look down and tell him, "It's down the hall, second door on the right."

Tasha runs and starts hitting Terry on the chest. "You just gonna let them take our son? You not gonna stop them?"

"Baby, I can't stop them. There's nothing we can do right now."

One police officer walks to the room. "Alex, I'm a police officer. I have to take you in." The police officer waits a couple seconds, then walks in. "Bud, I got to take you in. Don't be afraid, we gonna try to help you work this out." The police officer walks to Alex and gently picks him up.

Alex starts crying. "I didn't mean to! I didn't mean to!" As he walks out, Alex is walking, getting near the front door, and he starts to wonder and ask himself, *How can I do such a thing? What was I thinking! How did it make me feel?* "Mom, Mom, don't let them take me, Mom! Mom!"

"I'm sorry, baby. It's gonna be all right, just do as they say." Tasha turns around and holds her husband.

As they drive away, Alex looks out the window, crying. But should he? How would you feel in this situation?

*****

At Alice's house, Alice decides to call Beth.

"Hello."

"Hey, how you feeling?"

"I'm doing better, just keeping my mind off everything, trying to stay positive."

"That's good to hear. I shouldn't bother you with this then."

"No, you all right. What you need?"

"Well, I was sitting here thinking about the baby, and it came to me that I need a godmother or something like that."

Before Alice can say another word, Beth screams, "Yes! Yes, I'd love to help you take care of the baby. I didn't want to bring this up with everything that happened."

Meanwhile at the bar, Alesha sits listening to the listening device she put in Alice's house while watching the news about a man who got cleared of a murder due to lack of evidence, and the same judge who clears him is the judge who sent her to prison without letting the police investigate what happened when she was younger, even though the police gave the judge a reason investigate why Alesha killed her stepdad.

Alesha then thinks back to the days when her sister was being raped and how she always begged her mom to stop her stepdad. No matter how much her mom kicked and beat her, she still begged her to stop her stepdad, trying to help her sister in some type of way, fighting through the pain of endless beatings. She even offered herself to their stepdad, but he said she didn't have enough body and looks.

Alesha snaps out of her daydream and says under her breath, "The baby is innocent, so you have some time. Use it wisely."

*****

Beth and Alice are on the phone.

"I know, but we still got to move forward, and I'd loved to be in the baby's life. It can be good for me."

"Okay, that's good. Well, we'll talk again later."

"Okay, bye."

Alice rubs her stomach, smiling, proud of herself for getting away with what she did.

*****

Several months later, Alice, Beth, and Ben sit at the table having dinner when the doorbells rings. Alice is about to get up, but Ben tells her, "It's fine, I'll go get it. Hello, who is it?" Ben hear a lady and decides to open the door to see who it is. To his surprise, it's a lady and a teenage boy.

"I'm Isabelle, and this is my son, Jason."

"Jason? What—"

Before Ben can continue, Jason walks past Ben and goes into the dining room where he sees Beth and Alice laughing and talking.

Beth looks at Jason who's looking at Alice with an ugly expression of despise and anger. "Jason, is that you?"

"Beth, do you know him?"

"Yes, that's one of Tyler's friends."

Isabelle and Ben walk in and look at Jason, waiting to see what he says or does next. So are Beth and Alice.

"I came in to see how my biological mother, who dumped me off at the hospital like an unwanted dog, was doing! But it seems like she's doing just fine."

"Jason, stop! That's not how we planned this to go. Jason, what's gotten into you?"

"You ask her. Let her tell you how she had a baby and dropped it off because she didn't want it!"

Beth looks at Alice with a confused and surprised look. "How can it be? Alice? Is it true?"

Alice sits in the chair shaking, squeezing a glass cup till it breaks in her hand. "No! No! My baby died when I gave birth." Alice tries to stand up, but falls and grabs her stomach, crying. She says it again, but lower and sadder. "My baby died. How can you say such a thing?"

Everyone in the room looks at her with jaws dropping.

Beth grabs her hand that has some blood dripping from it and puts a towel on it. "You might have to go to the hospital."

"No! I'm fine."

"What do you mean? Can't you see she's pregnant and bleeding?"

"I know, but my son needs answers. It's okay, I'll tell you my tragic past."

Alice tells everyone how her mom was on drugs and how her stepdad always raped her but never touched her twin sister, how her sister did nothing to help her and only watched.

"He kept doing it and doing it, till one time they found out I was pregnant. During birth, I lost consciousness. When I woke back up, they said the baby didn't make it and didn't let me see. I'm sorry."

Isabelle, Jason's mom, hits Jason on the head. "Oh! I'm sorry too."

"Well, what happened after that?"

"Ben, hush!"

"No, it's all right. My mom overdosed, and my sister killed our stepdad, end of the story."

"That's enough. Let's go to the hospital and get your hand fixed up."

At the hospital room, the story continues.

"Isabelle, I'm not denying him, but can we get a blood test? I want to be sure about this."

"Sure. After hearing you out, I understand you don't wanna get hurt again."

Twenty minutes later, a doctor came in and told them that the test shows that Jason is her son, which brought tears to Alice's eyes. A pain that she could never let go released itself from her.

"Can I hug him?"

"Sure. Jason, give her a hug. I'm sure this is a lot for her. It was him that wanted to meet you. We will figure the rest out later, but I'm glad it worked out for y'all."

Beth and Ben, being overwhelmed because of Tyler, decide to leave.

"I hate to leave, Alice, but we have something else to take care of, if you don't mind."

Alice sniffles. "Okay, it's all right."

Jason sits next to Alice, talking.

After a little checkup, Isabelle takes Alice home and tells her they would be back another day. "Oh, do you need help with anything before we leave?"

"No, I'm all right. The pills they gave me working good. They might just put me out cold the rest of the night. Hey, but thank you. Y'all get on back before it gets too late."

*****

At a hotel, Alesha opens up a phone she bought at a gas station and texts Jackson.

UK: you ready to be the hand of god again and do what needs to be done

Jackson: where and when

UK: this time you gone handle it a lil' different make him feel more pains before you kill him.

Jackson: what's the name

UK: his name's bill, he was on the news for murder but got off due to lack of evidence but he's guilty I did the leg work

Jackson: I'll handle everything else

UK: keep it clean

Later that night, Jackson finds Bill's house and breaks in. Jackson hears a girl screaming and yelling, "Get off me, I'm done! Keep yo money!"

"It's too late, bitch! You gonna get it either way. Now stay still and take it."

"No, I don't want your nasty dick or money, you nasty pig."

Jackson sneaks behind Bill and knocks him out. "You clean up everything you brought or touch. Don't leave nothing."

"Okay, okay, thank you."

"Don't thank me, hurry up." Jackson looks around to make sure everything's clear, then puts Bill in the trunk.

Outside deep into the woods, Jackson carries the body and a hammer to an open area with flowers and throws Bill on the ground.

Bill wakes up and starts begging for his life. "What you want? I can give you anything."

"Did the girl you killed beg for her life? Didn't the girl you was about to rape beg you to stop!"

"You want money? I'll give you money, power. I'll help you get power. Please just don't kill me. I can change."

"I want justice. Justice for all the people you fucked up and over. Can you give me that, Bill?"

Before Bill lets any more sickening shit come out his mouth, Jackson tapes it shut, but Bill continues to try to talk.

Jackson kicks Bill back to the ground and screams, "I guess this God's will now!" And he swings the hammer toward his private area as hard as he can.

Bill screams as loud as he can with the tape over his mouth to the point of biting his tongue, bleeding through the tape, still rolling around on the ground.

"You need another one?" Jackson swings again and puts all his weight into it, hitting Bill between the legs again.

Bill lifts up and drops back down like a wet rag falling to the floor, damn near lifeless.

Oh no, no no no. It's not time to sleep."

Jackson breaks his legs and then moves to the arms. Bill wakes back up to pain, pain that brought him back from death's door, just to be thrown in a hole and buried alive—right next to the other five bodies (someone's been busy).

*****

Days later at Alice's house

"Jason, I'm about to go with Beth for a checkup. Do you wanna come?"

"I'm all right."

"Well, do you need anything?"

"Yeah, can you bring back some food from that new restaurant? I heard it has good food."

"Sure, come lock the door for me."

While in the living room watching TV, Jason looks at the back door and sees something shining on the floor. *I wonder what this is?* Jason picks the object up and realizes it's the earring he gave Tyler. *This can't be the earring I gave Tyler. He said he lost it over an older lady's house who he was hooking up with. He knew these meant a lot to me, so would he have lied? Oh, he probably left them over here when he came over. I heard he used to come over and help her out. What was I thinking just then?*

Later that night, he thought about how things have been going with Beth giving all her attention to Alice, then out of nowhere, a storm walked in.

Alesha walks through the door and sees Ben. "Well, if it ain't Ben. You must be the twin I heard so much about. Hope it's not all bad."

Alesha gets some drinks and sit in front of him.

"What you doing sitting at the bar alone looking all depressed? Let me guess, my cute perfect sister is slowly destroying your life. Well, she got a way of making shit work out."

"Why would you care if that was the case?"

"Well, because you don't know what you brought inside your family, Mr. Ben. It's pure poison. I'm surprised you lasted this long."

"From what I heard, you the poison evil twin."

"It's always like that when you only hear one side of the story, but who stopped to hear me out of listening to what I got to say? Sure is funny when I think about it. Y'all just playing her game right where she want y'all at."

"So you saying everything that Alice saying ain't true?"

"I didn't say that, but people got a way of twisting some things up because of the way they see it and refuse to see it any other way, and that's just damn wrong. Fuck up if you ask me, but hey, y'all don't ask."

"Well, right now, Alice is all my wife knows, and I'm about tired of it. She spends more time with Alice than me."

"Now ain't that crazy." Alesha takes one shot. "Well, Ben, my advice to you is to keep your eyes and ears open. You never know when the truth comes out, and it might just surprise everybody. Keep that in mind."

"It 'bout time for me to go."

"Well, let me buy a bottle and head to the house to drink alone."

Ben is in the house by himself, waiting on his wife, who seemed to take forever to come home.

"Baby, I'm home!" Beth takes her jacket off and heads to the living room where she sees Ben drinking. "You're drinking now? Well, I'm 'bout to head in."

Beth continues to walk, not paying Ben any mind.

Ben gets up and runs and grabs her. "Wait, you not gonna check on your husband or nuthin', just leave him alone in the dark?"

"I'm sorry, I been busy today. I wasn't thinking about it."

Ben kisses her on the neck. "I miss you, baby, where you been?"

"I been out with Alice."

Ben slowly rubs on her and kisses her more.

"I'm tired, Ben. I'm about to take a shower and go to sleep."

"Well, what about me? I need some attention too. We're moving farther apart. Sometimes I wonder if you're giving up."

Beth leaves Ben and walks to her room, not saying anything.

Ben walks outside, lights up a cigarette, and remembers what Alesha said about Alice. Ben lets out a little laugh and says, "I'll be damned" and continues to drink.

*****

In the hospital, Alice is lying on the bed, about to give birth.

"I'm gonna need you to push hard one more time for me."

Alice pushes as hard as she can till she hears a crying baby.

"It's a beautiful baby boy." The doctor cleans the baby up and hands him to Alice. "What you gonna name him?"

"Tyler. I'm gonna names him Tyler."

Beth walks in on Alice saying the baby boy's name. Beth laughs and runs over to get a look at baby Tyler. Beth and Ben hold the baby, and in both of their minds, they can see that the baby looks like Tyler a little, but they manage to keep a happy smile on their faces and return the baby back to Alice.

"Jason, come over and say hi to your baby brother. Y'all kinda look alike."

Jason sees the baby and smiles, but sees the baby looks familiar, like Tyler, which only furthers his suspicions.

Alice pretends like she don't know what they're thinking and makes a little joke. "Hey there, little man. I see you look like your cousin Tyler a little. I bet he would be happy to play with you."

"We're kin to Tyler?"

"Yes, but I don't know how yet, but for now, we'll just say y'all cousins."

Beth puts everything to the back of her mind and says, "That's right, we're all a big happy family."

Beth and Ben arrive at home with new thoughts and worries.

"So you gonna act like you didn't notice that and just go on with life as normal?"

"Ain't that the same thing you did? Didn't you want me to move on? Now that I'm moving on, you're making a big deal out of everything."

"For f—— sake, Beth, can you get it? I'm trying to pull this family together, but you won't let me. You'd rather hang with Alice and do God knows what. I saw her sister not too long ago, and she told me to watch out for Alice."

"You meeting with that killer? Are you having an affair too? Let me know, Ben."

"How dare you say that! I've been supporting you with all I have, and you been ignoring everything. That baby looks just like Tyler, and you're not suspicious at all? And don't say nu'n about them being family because we both know that ain't it, plus the unknown girl he was hooking up with and him visiting her one or two times. He was right in the middle of the fight between her and her husband. It just too much, Beth."

"I'm sorry, Ben, I know, I know."

"You still not listening! Hold on, wait, you what?"

"I know, Ben. I didn't involve you in this because you thought I was just trying to hold on to him and not move on. Why you think I'm trying to get close to her and doing all this?"

"We can't go to the police because we don't have evidence. Hell, we don't got nothing, and should we even bother? What good would it do?"

"Tyler's gone. If that is his baby, it would only be hurting him, so I say we find a way to take it, regardless of what happened or how it happened."

"Okay, Beth, you lead the way. I'll back you up with whatever you want. I haven't had your back, but you got my full support now."

"Okay, and what's this talk about Alesha?"

"I was at the bar one night, and she showed up. She basically said not to trust Alice, that the truth would come out someday."

"Was she talking about Alice having an affair with our Tyler, or was she talking about something bigger?"

"I don't know, but I do know there's something else that we don't know, and Alesha ain't completely bad."

"Okay, we need to set up a meeting to meet with her one day. We can't do this alone."

"What about Jason? Won't all of this hurt him too in the end?"

"It probably would, but like you said, it's time for us to get back together on track. We can't worry about other people's kids. We can't worry about other kids when we might have our own."

*****

Alesha pulls up to Alice's house and knocks on the door.
"Who is it?"
"Alesha. It's your sister whose life you destroyed with yo lies."
Jason opens the door and sees his aunt for the first time.
Alesha sees Jason and freezes up. She gently reaches her hands out touch his face. "You grew up into a wonderful boy." Alesha has a memory of her saving Jason when her stepdad was about to kill him. "Saving you was worth it."
While Alesha holds Jason's face, a tear drops down, and Jason jumps away.
"You my evil aunt who watched my mom get beat and did nothing and killed y'all stepdad in cold blood."
"Is that what that lying perverted —— said? Well, she only told one side of that half-true story she made up." Alesha walks away while saying, "I'm pretty sure you already see some of the skeletons in her closet."
Alesha drives away and pulls out another burner phone she has prepared and texts Jackson.

UK: it's time to bring down the hammer of justice
Jackson: you have another evil person that needs to be killed
UK: a judge that lets evil go on and does nothing to stop it, Judge Waller
Jackson: consider it done
UK: handle him in his house as always keep it clean and don't make mistakes.

*****

Jackson watches Waller's every move for two days and stakes out his house.

Waller is on the phone with someone, talking as if he's above everybody. "These fools think I care about being fair or providing justice. The only thing I care about is making money off them and ruling over them with a iron fist. Hahaha!" Waller lets out a lazy laugh. "You should try it out, it's a fun game."

Waller hangs up the phone and goes to sleep, not knowing what awaits him.

Jackson sneaks into his house through a window he left open due to his arrogance. Jackson puts a rag over his face then knocks him out when he tries to get up.

Tied to a chair with tape over his mouth, Waller opens his eyes and tries to get loose.

"Well well well, the king wakes."

Waller continues to shake the chair till he sees Jackson pointing to the right of his head where he has a pole with a knife pointed at his head.

"I wouldn't shake too much. Don't wanna end it too fast, do you? All right, Judge the Great Ruler. Choose from that knife or the flame that will burn your sins away!"

Jackson pours gas all around him and Waller, then lights a candle beside him.

"The timer is set. You choose."

Jackson then leaves the house, leaving him to his own fate.

*****

The next morning at Alice's house, Alice is sitting down with the baby, singing to him. "Go to sleep, go to sleep, go to sleep, my little Tyler. Go to sleep, go to sleep, go to sleep, my little Tyler." She then looks at the floor and says, "I wish you could have met your daddy, but it just wasn't meant to be."

*****

Inside a black Range Rover, a man is on the phone.

"Don't worry, I'm gone have your money, just don't hurt my family. I'm gone have your man, just give me some time."

"How you gone get me my money, Jake?"

"I have a daughter whose husband died. She stays in a big house, and I'm sure she got some money off him."

The stranger is laughing loudly. "Now that's low, Jake. You gonna take money from your daughter you abandoned to keep your other family safe? Even I wouldn't go that far."

"Do you want your money?"

"Of course."

Then don't worry about how I get the money!"

"I'll be looking for you soon. Have my money, Jake."

*****

Meanwhile, Beth and Ben are at a restaurant.

"Here's your food, sir. Everything else will be out soon."

Ben looks up and is surprised by who it is. "Alesha, is that you? You're working at a restaurant?"

"Yes, sir. I'm working right now, but I'm free later." Alesha walks back to the back and looks at a chef in a lustful way.

"That was Alesha. It's amazing how much they look alike!"

"Well, they are twins. Get some paper and write our numbers on it. We need to talk to her."

Ben writes his and Beth's number down and hands it to Alesha when she comes back out.

"I can't believe we're having our own baby."

"Yes, all everything will work out for the best baby."

"I know you probably don't want to, but I think we should visit Alex's parents."

"If that's what you wanna do, than we should do it. It might help us all."

*****

At Alice's house, Jake sits outside in the car, getting ready to go in. Jake knocks on the door.

"Who is it?"

"It's Jake, your father."

Alice thinks back and remembers her mom saying Jake was her father, then walks to the door, not knowing what to say, confused. "Who are you?"

"I'm your father."

"No, I didn't have a father going through that hell I went through. So who are you, and what you want?"

"Look, I didn't come here to argue or make any problems. I'm not asking for forgiveness. I just wanna get involved in y'all lives before it's too late. I wanted a father growing up but never got one and still don't got one, so I guess we both out of luck."

The baby starts crying.

"I have to go, my baby is crying."

"I hear a baby. I'm guessing I have a little grandson."

"You have nothing!" She than slams the door in his face and walks to the baby.

*****

Alesha is at work and is about to leave, talking to one of her coworkers named Fillip.

"Hey, Alesha. I was wondering if you wanted to come over my place and eat dinner?"

"Umm, I guess so, it depends on what you cooking."

"Don't worry, I cook your favorite, mashed potatoes with mushroom gravy and steak slices."

"You sure know how to please a girl. If I knew better, I'd say this a date."

"Well, if you want it to be, I wouldn't mind."

"It's not that easy, Fillip. See you in a couple hours."

Alesha gets in her car and takes out her burner phone and texts Jackson.

UK: update me

Jackson: some man in a Range Rover showed up and said he was her father

She went off on him an slammed the door.

UK: did you get a license plate?

Jackson: yeah

Jackson: I already know something up with her she's not clean and you wouldn't have me spying on her for nothing, so why don't we just take her out

UK: you will do nothing without my ok, don't go messing everything up because you're feeling yourself

UK: an as of now I don't know if she killed anyone so you wait and listen to my order

*****

Jackson is looking at his phone and sees the Range Rover pull back up and also another car. In the other car, it's Jason getting dropped off to spend summer break with Alice.

"Have fun, baby."

"I will, Mom."

Jackson and Jason meet up at the door. "Who are you, young man?"

Jason looks at him with an irritated look. "I'm someone who's staying here. Who are you?"

Jackson gets in the car, texting UK, telling everything that's happening.

Jason takes out a key Alice gave him and heads in.

Jake walks behind him, but Jason closes the door in his face and locks it. "Alice, there's a strange man outside the door."

Alice walks toward Jason. "Here, get your brother."

Jake outside hears them because he had his ear to the door.

"What do you want?"

"That must be my other grandson?"

Before Jake can say anything, Alice repeats, "What do you want!" in a more frustrating force.

"I came to see do you know where your sister stays at nowadays? I'm trying to see what I missed out on and learn about y'all lives."

Alice puts her thinking face on, then says, "Well, come in."

Jackson is still in the car.

Uk: ok that's all you can leave

*****

Alesha is standing in her room, getting ready to leave. *That sly fox switched up fast. She don't want my side of the story getting around and hurting her fake little image she built.*

Jackson starts to wonder about a couple things, then calls Alesha's phone.

Alesha answers, "Hello."

Jackson says, "It's been a while. I wanted to tell you, word around town is your father's in town."

"I have no father, and even if such a person was here, how would you know?"

"I got my connection."

Alesha gets mad. "You're still looking into my life? First you get aggressive and harass me, don't contact me for god knows how many months, now you call harassing me again! I should just call the police and have them investigate you. How would you like that?"

"Hold up, hold up, that's not called for. You don't have to go that far. I won't mess with you again."

"You think it's that easy? No, you owe me."

"What you want?"

"Look up that man and give me whatever you find."

Jackson laughs. "Okay."

Alesha heads toward Fillip with a smile of love.

Knock knock knock.

"I'm coming, one second."

"Don't have a woman waiting, Fillip. This your only shot, don't miss it," she says with a smile on her face.

Fillip opens the door while saying, "Okay, well, I'll make sure to wow you."

Alesha walks in feeling happy for the first time in a long time.

"Take your jacket off. You can hang it where you want. You can sit in the living or dining room, whichever one suits you. Get as comfortable as you can be. I'll be right back, my lady."

Fillip brings a plate to her.

"Enjoy, my queen."

"My favorite! You're spoiling me already."

Alesha covers her mouth and talks. "This is good. You know what, we should open our own restaurant."

"Our own? You said that like we a couple."

"Well, I thought that what you was aiming for."

"Well, I guess that makes it official."

They hear someone knocking at the door.

"Coming, who is it?"

"It's your baby momma. Now open up! Let me come in." She pushes her way in while pulling a little girl behind her. "Oh, it smelling good in here. What you cooking, Fillip?"

"Stop, stop. Why you always doing this shit?" Fillip looks down and says, "I'm sorry, baby girl. Daddy and Momma having a problem."

"You much got a ***** in here, I know you do. I can smell her. She must be white, that some white girl perfume."

"Can you please stop? Not today, you can't mess this up for me."

"Look at this in here having dinner with a fine *** white girl. Well, guess what, now y'all got a family because it's your turn to keep your baby. It's time for me to do me and get mines together."

Alesha gets up. "Fillip, it was nice, but I think I need to go and let you handle this. I'll see my way out."

"Oh, I like her. You got you a good one, I see."

Fillip says okay with a disappointed look.

"Why you looking like your dog died?" Alesha walks over to Fillip, grabs his shirt, pulls closer, and gives him the kiss of his life, then walks away as if it didn't happen. "We'll talk tomorrow."

"So you just gonna drop our daughter off and leave?"

"Yeah, watch me."

The baby mamma walks out the house and leaves.

Fillip goes to the room and talks to his daughter, Bella. "Well, Bella, looks like you gonna be with Daddy from now own."

Bella jumps toward Fillip and hugs him. "I like Daddy. Momma was mean to me."

*****

Days later at Alice's house

"So what do you really want? I know you didn't come here to catch up."

"You're right, I didn't. I need some money. I owe some people some money."

"I knew you didn't care about me or my sister. So how much?"

"15,000."

"If I give it to you, will you leave and never come back?"

"You'll never see my face again."

Alice walks to her room and opens a safe with saved-up money in it. "Here, this all the money James saved up. Take it and leave."

Alesha, who ended back over Fillip's, wakes up beside him to her phone ringing.

"Hey, sounds like you had a long night. Somebody must got busy lately."

"I decided to try and better my life. It's going good so far, lots of new stuff, if you know what I mean."

"So you giving up on putting away your sister after what she did to you?"

Alesha gets up and finds a quiet place to talk. "Why can't you just be happy for me? I'm finally finding love."

"No, of course I'm happy, but we can't just leave her alone with Tyler and Jason. They cannot be left with her."

"Well, what do you wanna do because I see no other option right now."

"I have a plan. We need to get under her skin and get her to do something, make her slip up."

"This is a dangerous game you're playing Beth. This can go wrong very fast. You know Alice can be unpredictable. Plus, you have your baby to think about too now. We have to really think this through."

"I have to do this for my baby's future too. I can't let his nephew be raised by such a person."

"Okay, what's the plan?"

"We gone start off by having dinner together, all of us."

"You sure?"

"Yes, don't tell your part of the story, just go with the flow."

"All right, I'll be over later then."

Fillip sneaks up and grab her from behind. "Who you talking on the phone with?"

Alesha takes Fillip's hand and puts it on her stomach. "My friend Beth. She wants me to come to dinner with her later."

"Well, have fun."

"Since I'm feeding three people now, I'll have to eat a little more."

"How you feeding three people, fatty?"

"Me and the twins." Alesha rubs Fillip's hands on her stomach.

Fillip stops and spins Alesha around. "Are you for real?"

"Well, we have been hooking up for a while now, and you don't like using protection, so it's on you."

"I know we good at keeping secrets, and only losers use protection I like to feel everything."

"Well, you gonna have to become a loser, can't have too many."

"Let me go take a shower and get ready for my day."

At Beth's house later that day, Alice, Jason, baby Tyler, Ben, and Beth sit at the table, talking and laughing.

"Alice, I don't want you to get mad at what I'm 'bout to tell you. Can you promise me you'll approach this with an open mind?"

Everyone gets quiet, waiting to hear what Beth is bringing up.

"Beth, what do you want to say?"

"I've talked to Alesha a few times."

"You've what! After I told you how I felt about her!"

"I know. I think she changed and wants to put the past behind her and build a relationship with her sister and nephew. I lost my son, so I know how important family is."

"You could have asked me before you went sticking your nose in my business."

"Hold on, Alice. Now you're being a lil' too hostile. We just invited her over because she's nice to us and looks like a good person. Everyone deserves a second chance at life. I thought you out of everything would understand that."

Alice, feeling cornered, can only say, "Well, don't say I didn't warn y'all."

"I think this will be good for your family, but mostly for Tyler and Jason."

"I don't mind." Alice looks at Jason with a nasty expression and changes it as fast as she can, thinking no one saw it, so she put on a smile.

Jason is frightened a little, but manages to cover it up.

Ben and Beth finally see the ugliness Alesha sees.

Knock knock knock.

"I'm coming!" Beth opens the door and invites Alesha in. "Come in, have a seat. I'll fix you some to eat."

"Hello, everyone."

Alice turns her head, dissatisfied with everyone, including her own son. "Hey."

"Hey, Alesha."

"Show some respect and call her Auntie Alesha or aunt."

"Okay. Hey, Auntie Alesha."

"Oh, he all right, but thank you, Ben and Jason."

Beth brings some food and tells her to dive in. "Do you want any wine?"

"No, but thank you, everyone, and the food looks very good."

"So how's it going at the restaurant?"

"It's going good. Me and Fillip talking about opening our own up."

Alice humphs under her breath. "Oh, is that your new man who keeps you busy all night?"

"We actually been seeing each other for a while now."

"You kept it a secret that long."

"Yeah, I really like him and wanted to take it slow with letting everybody know."

Alice humphs again.

"Okay, let me start off by saying I'm sorry, Alice. I'm sorry I didn't do enough to protect you."

Before Alesha can finish, Alice screams, "How dare you come in here with your pathetic apology!" Alice gets so mad that she throws a glass cup at Alesha's head.

Glass goes everywhere and toward the baby beside Beth, but she reacts fast enough to move the baby.

"Alice, what's you problem? You could have hurt the baby."

"I'm sorry, I didn't mean to."

"No, you have to leave and think about your actions."

Alice gets up and walks toward the baby.

"You think you are getting this baby after that? You can leave!"

"I'm sorry, I don't know what came over me, please."

"No! Leave now and think about what you did in front of the baby and Jason."

Alice starts walking away, and Jason gets up too.

"You sit back down. You staying here too! Jason, you can sleep in Tyler's room tonight if it's not too uncomfortable for you."

"It's okay. I'd like to sleep in there."

"You can get some of his old clothes."

Beth, Alesha, and Ben continue talking.

"That convinced me that we really do need to do something about her."

"I told y'all how unpredictable she is. She's dangerous and willing to do anything when she backed into a corner."

"I'm sorry, Alesha. I brought you back into this mess. I know you trying to build a life."

Meanwhile, in the hall listening is Jason. He hears they whole conversation and asks himself what can he do.

"No, she's my responsibility too. I can't let her destroy Jason's life. I didn't get beaten to death saving his life for him to be broken by her. I refuse to let her win."

Jason, with a confused face, steps back and walks back to the room and calls someone.

"You lied to me, and Alice is a horrible person."

"I didn't lie, I just wasn't fully honest because it's a lot I'm not proud of, and I didn't say she was a good person. I just gave you the means to find her and figure out yourself."

Jason hangs up on the person and goes to sleep angry at how his mother turned out to be.

A few days later, Alice came to Beth's house to pick up her baby and Jason. "I was out of line, and I'm sorry for everything. I know there's no excuse for how I acted."

"It's all right, you just needed a break."

"Hey, do you want to go out later?"

"I wish I could, but Alesha said she had something important to tell me."

"Oh, it's all right, maybe another time. Well, did she say what she had to tell you?"

"No, not really. She said something about the honest truth. Guess I'll figure out when I go."

Alice leaves with a nervous look, wondering what her sister got planned.

"You think she bought it?"

"I know she did, Ben."

Later that evening, Beth's phone rings. "Hello."

"Yes, this is Dr. Levi from the hospital. I was going over some old cases and came across Tyler's case and an autopsy. Well, this hard to say, but I see that Tyler had a strain on his lungs that might have caused his death."

"That can't be right."

Ben walks through the door from outside.

"Tyler had good lungs. He never had any problems breathing or anything for that matter."

"Well, I don't know where you should go from here, but I was just making sure you know."

Beth hangs up the phone with a look of shock and anger.

"What was that about?"

Beth explains to Ben what the doctor said.

"No, I know what you thinking. No she wouldn't. Why would she?"

"To stop him from coming clean about the affair. It adds up when you think about it."

"I pray not. I hope she's not that far gone."

"Well, we will work it out tomorrow. You need some rest. Take care of that baby, my baby." Ben kisses Beth on the neck while rubbing her stomach.

"Stop, baby. You ready for another one already? This one ain't out yet."

At Alice's house, Alice gets her baby bag, goes upstairs into the safe, and grabs money and a gun. Alice puts the money and gun into the baby bag and yells for Jason.

"Yeah, you need some?"

"No, me and the baby about to go out real quick to buy some things. Do you need anything from the store before they close?"

"No, I'm good. I'm about to go to sleep."

Alice leaves the house with a face of a tiger out to kill its prey.

Jason runs to her room and starts looking around and opens the closet door to find a picture of Alesha with a knife in it and takes a picture of it.

"Oh my god," Jason says as he looks at the wall scared because he doesn't know what type of person he's staying with.

Alice pulls up to a group of people and lets the window down. "Hey, can I speak to y'all?"

The group walks over. "Yo, what you need?"

Alice shows a picture to the group. "I need her killed. Here's $5,000. I'll come back here with another $5,000 when you do the job."

"Do you know where she be?"

"Yeah, here's her address. Call me when you finish."

"You better bring the other half when it's done, or you gonna have some problem. Can y'all believe this? She wants her own sister killed."

The next morning, Ben and Beth visit Alesha at Fillip's house.

"Come in. Fillip's gone, and Bella is playing in her room."

Beth and Ben explain what they heard from the doctor and what they think.

"Well, it's very possible. That's why we have to be more careful. This is not a game, it's getting dangerous, and I don't want nobody else getting hurt because of my crazy sister."

Ben looks at the TV and sees the news on. "Hey, turn that up. I been hearing about that."

The news reporter states, "This is Rebecca reporting from a clearing deep within the woods." She puts her head down and lifts it back up. "I never thought I'd see something like this. There seems to be at least thirty bodies buried out here killed in horrible ways. I think this is connected to the missing people lately."

Beth and Alesha cover their mouths, speechless.

"What has the world come to? It's something new every day. When you got people doing horrible stuff like this, how can you live life without looking over your shoulder?"

Beth and Ben start getting up.

"Be safe and watch out, Alesha. Nowhere's safe anymore. I'm thinking about getting a gun."

"Oh, hush, Ben. What you know about guns?"

Ben and Beth leave while talking to each other about the gun and how Ben felt.

"Well, what should we do now?"

"I think we should slow down and plan this out more because I don't think she'll come after us. But Alesha, that's another story."

"You're right. I got a little carried away thinking about the kids and not about Alesha and the risk she's taking."

*****

Alice is at home sitting down with the baby in the living room.

Jason looks at Alice with a pale face.

"Jason, what's wrong you? You been a little distant."

Jason stares at Alice, his shirt open a little, and reveals a hand mark around his neck.

"I had to, Jason. I thought you was gone tell, but I see you're not, so all is forgiven." Alice continues to sing and hold the baby.

*****

At Fillip's house

"I'm home! Where my babies at!"

Bella jumps up out of Alesha's lap. "In here, Daddy!" Bella runs to Fillip and gets picked up.

"There you go, my Princess Bella. Babe, I left the food in the car. Let me go get it, I'll be right back."

"No, I'll go get it. You relax. I know your shift's usually harder." Alesha walks out to the car and opens the car door.

Behind her, three people start jumping on her and hitting her.

"Stop, stop! Fillip, help!"

Fillip hears them and goes to his bed to grab his gun. Finally making it through the door, Fillip sees one of the people point a gun at Alesha and shoots her in the arm.

Fillip starts to shoot at the three. One got hit two times, and the other two make it out.

Alesha is holding her stomach, not worrying about the gunshot wound. She calls Fillip. Fillip runs to Alesha and calls the police while he holds Alesha.

The police finally make it. "We got it from here, sir. Go get your daughter."

"She's pregnant with twins."

The other paramedic goes to one of the gang members. This one is still alive, but barely.

Fillip grabs Bella and gets in the car to follow the ambulance.

Fillip calls Beth.

"Hello?"

Fillip talks fast.

"Slow down, Fillip. What happened?"

"They shot her. They jumped on her and shot her."

"Do you know who or why?"

"No, but I'm following the ambulance."

"Oh my god. Okay, keep me updated. We're about to head that way too."

"What happened?"

Beth tells Ben what happened.

"You think this is a coincidence?"

"I don't think so. We both know who might be behind this. It's our fault."

On the way to the hospital, the man who was shot dies.

At the hospital, Alesha opens her eyes.

"Baby, you okay?" Fillip grabs her hand and rubs her face while calling for the doctor.

"She seems to be all right."

Beth and Ben walk in with shameful faces.

"Don't y'all dare look like this. This not y'all fault. I choose to help y'all."

"Help them? Alesha, what you talking about? So this wasn't a random attack?"

Alesha kisses Fillip while whispering, "I'll tell you when we settle down back at home."

"Come and stay at my house for a couple days and rest."

"That's a good idea. The babysitter can keep Bella when I'm at work. You need to heal physically and emotionally."

Alesha cries and kisses Fillip. "I love you."

"I love you too, honey."

"Okay, Beth."

A couple days later, Alesha and Beth sit around talking.

"I don't think we can do this on our own anymore. I think we should get the police involved."

"I think so too. I lost one of my babies because of this madness. I just know this happened because of her."

Knock knock knock.

"Who is it?"

"It's Alice."

"I'm coming." Beth lean toward Alesha, who begins to get mad. "Calm down. We can't do nothing right now, and we don't wanna start anything. We can't handle this no more. Let's just act like somebody tried to rob you."

"Okay, but tomorrow, we're going to the police station."

Beth walks to the door and lets Alice in.

"Hey, Beth, how you doing today?"

"I'm fine, just helping Alesha make it through her hard times."

Alice shows a surprised look. "What happened?"

Beth explains what happened.

"That's tragic. I wouldn't wish that on no one!" She walks toward Alesha. "I'm so sorry you had to go through that. I know it's nothing I can do and we have our problems, but as a sister, I'm here for you." Alice looks at Beth. "Beth taught me that."

"Where's Jason, Alice?"

"Oh, he's gone. His mom came and picked him up, they had somewhere to go, I guess."

"When will they be back?"

"I don't know at the moment."

"Well, you still got that little handsome guy."

"He keeps me busy all day. I'm not gonna butt in on y'all time. Let me get baby Tyler home."

Next day, Beth and Alesha are pulling up to the police station. Alesha sees Jackson leaving.

"Hey, Alesha and…?"

"This is my friend Beth."

"Nice to meet you, Miss Beth. Is there anything I can help y'all with?"

"No, we're fine."

"Okay, well, be safe."

"How do you know him?"

"He wanted to investigate my sister's case. I guess he thought something didn't seem right about it. Something about the way Tyler looked, like there was something more to the accident."

"Oh really? That's interesting." Beth shows Alesha the text of Tyler and Jason.

"What could it be?"

"I don't know. He died before telling anyone, but we have to get Jason and the baby away from her."

Beth and Alesha sit down at a desk.

"Well, ma'am, I'm sorry to tell you, but we can't do anything yet or right now. I need some more solid. Bring me something I can use. I can't build a case off of what y'all just telling me."

"Y'all can at least take a look into this! People's lives in danger. It's y'all job to look into it."

"We can't investigate a person's life because of hunches and she say, he say. Now you can go to the child protection program and talk to them to have them check and see if the environment is bad for the kids."

"Never mind then. I see why people say y'all useless. Y'all rather wait till someone dead and pretend like y'all tried to help. Let's go, Alesha. This was a waste of time."

Beth and Alesha walk toward the car.

"Can you believe this? They ignoring us because we lack *proof* proof. I don't know what else we can do, she's too smart to get caught making a mistake. We need to find a way to catch her red-handed. Let's go home and think about it. I don't think she gonna do anything right now."

At Alice's house, she packs a little bag, a gun, and some money. Alice throws the stuff in the car with the baby while mumbling, "They not gone take you from me. They took Jason, but not you. They can't get you, my little Tyler. They will have to catch me first. I won't go down. We won't go down, my baby."

Beth and Alesha make it home.

"Honey, we're home. It didn't go as planned."

Ben is at the house watching TV, wondering how the killing they heard of will turn out. "Sorry I couldn't go, but what did they say?"

"There's nothing they can do right now. We have to figure something out. I feel like we're running out of time."

Someone knocks on Beth's door in a light manner.

"I'm coming. One second please." Beth opens the door slowly to see who it is.

"I'm looking for Alice or her sister. Is any one of them here?"

"Do you need them for something?"

"Yes, I'm their mother, Jasmine. I'm trying to see them and work some family problems out."

Alesha hears what the old lady says and stands up.

"I know their mother passed away, so you can't be."

"Let me in, I can explain."

"Let her in. We don't want someone hearing us and bringing more trouble."

Jasmine walks in. She makes eye contact with Alesha, and she walks toward her. "My daughter, my beautiful daughter! I'm so sorry for failing you."

Alesha looks in disbelief. "Mom, no! But you're dead!" Alesha's face gets red as she gets mad. "You're supposed to be dead! You should be dead!"

Beth runs over to Alesha. Alesha is breathing heavily, getting weak.

"Alesha, calm down. The baby, Alesha. You have to calm down. Jasmine, can you step out so we can calm her down?"

Ben sits Alesha down on the couch. "Breathe, Alesha, slowly. We don't want you passing out."

"Ben, go get my pills. She should be able to take them to help her calm down."

Ben returns with a pill and water.

"Alesha, take these. They will help you calm down. I know you want to know how she's here."

"Yes, I'm okay now. I wasn't ready for that. So much anger and pain overwhelmed me."

"Can I bring her back in?"

"Yes, I'm fine."

"Ben, go to the door and let Jasmine in!"

"No small talk. I want to know how you still alive."

"That night I told the ambulance that was able to save me, I was in no shape to take care of y'all, so they took y'all. I'm sorry for everything I did to you. You protected your sister and was punished, and I couldn't do anything. I won't ask for forgiveness, but let me at least show y'all I'm a better person. Alesha? Alesha, where's your sister and nephew? I went over her place but couldn't find them."

Alesha sniffles. "How you know where they stay and about Beth?"

"I spent a lot of time tracking y'all down and getting myself together. I also told Jason about y'all. That's how he got to meet y'all. So where are they?"

"Alice said Jason's mom came and got him the last time we saw her."

"No, that can't be. I just talked to his mother not too long ago, and she said he hasn't answered his phone. That's one of the reasons why I came."

"What's that crazy bitch done? I just know she up to something."

"Ben, let's go over her house and see if she if she made it back. That's if she coming back, but we can see if she left anything too."

Everyone gets in the car and drives to Alice's house in a hurry because something doesn't feel right.

Ben walks to the door as fast as he can without bringing attention to them.

"Hey, someone call her and see if she answers."

"No, she didn't answer. The phone is off. Ben, knock the door in. We'll just say we was worried because she disappeared."

Ben kept hitting the door till he finally got it to open.

"Is that an alarm?"

"Yeah, that's an alarm. Hurry it up."

"What's wrong? Why y'all doing all this?"

"Alice went crazy."

"No, I say her ass been crazy. Look for anything, anything at all."

Everybody meets back in the living room after looking.

"I didn't find anything."

"Wait one second, didn't Alice say something about having a basement?"

"Yeah, I remember."

Ben runs to the basement and doesn't see nothing but junk and a freezer. Ben looks closer and sees a shirt hanging out it. "Please don't be that, please don't be that." Ben repeats the same thing over and over. "Shit, this is scary. How do people do it?" Ben opens the freezer. "Oh my god, no! How could she do this to her own son?"

Beth, Jasmine, and Alesha run in and see what Ben is looking at.

"What is this? Jason! Jason! I know she did it. We couldn't protect him."

"For lord's sake, you saying your sister did this, Alesha?"

"That's not all she did, that twisted, crazy bitch! She destroys everything she touches. I think I hear the police."

Ben is outside talking to the police. "Yes, sir. We couldn't contact her and felt like something was off. My wife tried to talk to the police about her, but they didn't pay her any attention."

"I'm sure they had their reasons, sir. You and your wife can leave. We don't need y'all at the moment. We will bring y'all in if we have questions."

"Ben, what did he say?"

"They don't care where they don't need us, so we have to leave."

"But we have more to say."

"I know, baby. Let's just leave."

Meanwhile Jasmine is on the phone, telling Jason's mother what happened.

"I'm sorry, Isabelle. We don't know what happened. They got to investigate."

"Investigate what? He was at Alice's house. Where is Alice?"

"I don't know right now, but I don't think it's her fault. Besides, he was her son."

"Oh, okay, Jasmine. I will get to the bottom of this. Your family will pay if it's her doing."

Chapter 2

"Alice, did you hear me? Alice?"

"Yes, I heard you. I just need time to process this. Do y'all need any help? I'm about to go back home."

"Oh no, we're all right. You need time to come to terms with everything."

"Ben, you think she gonna be all right? I wonder what she gonna do now."

"Only time will tell. We just got to wait and help her build a new life."

"I thought I just saw Alesha in a white coat."

"You're just tired and need some rest. You can go home. I'll stay here."

*****

In the room sitting in darkness with a creepy smile on his face, Alex thinks about how he shot Tyler, how it made him feel. He said it was a mistake, but to him, it didn't feel like one. It almost felt natural. He tried not to do it, but at the same time, he let it happen and felt a release of stress. This feeling of power is something he can get used to.

"Doctor, Doctor, he's waking up."

A doctor rushes in the room and checks his vitals. "Well, it looks like everything's fine, good blood flow, strong heart. With some rest at home, he'll make a full recovery. Just take it easy, and don't strain yourself for a couple days. You'll be good."

In the car heading home the next day, after getting discharged from the hospital, Tyler thinks of the horrible dream he had. He thought about telling his mom, but she'll probably say he needs to see a therapist, but he still has the problem with Alice and wants to come clean about everything, but maybe him getting shot was a warning that he shouldn't and just keep everything in.

"Hey, Tyler, what you thinking 'bout? You been zoned out. Do you need somebody to talk to about what happened?"

"Oh, no, Mom. I'm good. I just had some on my mind, but it's nothing."

"Okay, but if you need help, just tell me. I know you can't do anything right now, but if Alice needs some help later on when you're feeling better, make sure to help her if you can because she is pregnant, but don't go around talking about it."

When Tyler heard those words, his heart nearly stopped beating, damn near swallowing his tongue. *How can I, at such a young age, get into so much shit?*

Beth and Tyler walk up to the door.

"What's wrong, Tyler? I thought you'll be happy to be home."

"I'm happy but just a little nervous."

As they walk through the door, they get a big surprise and a welcome-home cheer. Tyler knows he has to put a smile on his face before everyone sees something bothering him and says thank you.

"Come and get some to eat, Tyler."

Tyler walks over to the table where he sees Alice and waves at her. The first thing that popped into his head is *Holy shit, I did that.*

Meanwhile, over Fillip's house, Alesha thinks about the feelings she has for Fillip and about the things she already did that would hurt him if she found out. She is willing to give up her revenge for him and give him her whole heart.

"Babe, I'll be back. I have an important call I need to take, and I'm going out for real quick. Do you need anything?"

Walking outside, Fillip gets a call from an unknown number. "Hello, who is this?"

"Don't worry about that. The only thing you need to worry about is keeping your girlfriend out of jail for murder and helping make a serial killer."

"What the hell you talking about? I will call the police!"

Ding!

Fillip gets a text and opens it where he sees a video of Alesha and the police in the woods.

"What do you want?"

"I want your money, $20,000. I know you got it since you got your own restaurant now."

"I don't have that type of money yet. I can get you $10,000 up front."

"Give me the $10,000 and the other $10,000 when you get it, but don't wait too long. I got this video."

Fillip walks in the house and watches Alesha play with his daughter and sees how happy the two of them are. He knows he has to do whatever it takes to protect them in any way he can.

At Tyler's house, Jason and his mom pull up to see how he's doing. Ben comes to the door and lets them in. "Come in, he's right over there."

Jason and Isabelle walk toward Tyler till they see a face they didn't think they would see. Jason looks at Alice for a while without saying a word till Alice asks if he needs anything.

"I'm sorry. He was a little surprised because you might be his biological mother. I adopted him when he was a baby. He wanted to see his biological mother, so we used his blood and ran it through the system, looking for anyone related to him and look like him. Your name and picture happened to show up."

Everyone in the room is in shock at what they are hearing because Alice once told them some of her past, but no one was as surprised as Tyler. He can't believe this. *Shit, what's next in this shit show?*

Alice thinks about things before she says anything and works it out in her head. She learned from her mistakes of going off before thinking. "Okay, I understand."

"Well, this can be good, Alice. You found out Tyler and me related to you, now you might have your son."

"Hold up, wait, we're related?"

"Oh yeah, you was in that little coma, so you didn't hear we're related to Alice some type of way. I don't know how for real because our family had a few problems."

Tyler thinks to himself, *So wait a minute. I fuck a grown lady who turns out to be related to me, and she's my best friend's mom. Let's not forget, she's pregnant, and nine times out if ten, it's by me. Well, who said life can be boring?*

The next day, everyone gets together and goes to the hospital and finds out Jason really is Alice's son. After that, they have a talk about some of the things that happened and how they wanted to proceed.

"Well, it's up to Jason if he wants to get to know you. I won't stop him."

"I don't mind, Mom, but I don't want to move or anything."

"Big head, I'm not talking about moving, just staying over sometimes. Plus, you got Tyler nearby too."

"Okay, I don't mind. Can I stay over Tyler's this weekend?"

"You'll have to ask his mom."

"Oh, he can stay. Tyler needs the company anyway."

At Fillip's house, Fillip picks Alesha up and drops her on the bed.

"Ah, bad boy! I like it when you get rough."

"Oh, you like that, huh? I got more where that come from. I know you not used to this. When I get finished, you now gone want to leave."

Alesha takes her hand and grabs Fillip's dick. "I never thought about leaving any."

Fillip takes her clothes off and gently kisses her on her neck while just barely rubbing her nipple and putting his hand in her pussy, curving his finger up in her, vibrating his finger till he gets a pleasurable moan out of her.

"Don't stop, don't stop. It feels so good." Alesha lifts her body in the air, almost climaxing till Fillip stops. "No, don't stop." Alesha grabs Fillip's face and pulls him to her. "I want that."

"Oh, you want what?"

"I want this." Alesha pushes Fillip on the bed and hops on him. She rubs his dick on her pussy, slowly pushing it in, letting out a moan that shows how beautiful she is even if you couldn't see her; just hearing her moans would mesmerize you.

Alesha rides Fillip, trying not to take in too much, feeling so good from the pleasure that she falls on his chest. Fillip grabs her and flips her back over, then grabs her waist, lifting her up, and starts pumping while leaning back. "Ah, ah, I'm 'bout to cum hard…hard." Fillip starts pumping harder and faster till Alesha cums. Fillip feels her wet warm juices, pulls out, and cums on her stomach.

Fillip and Alesha take their showers. Alesha lies down, but Fillip puts some clothes on to take the money to the blackmailer. He kisses her on the head and tells her he's going out with some friends.

"Okay, baby. I'm about to go to sleep, I'm tired."

Fillip laughs. "I bet you are not used to that."

Alesha laughs and turns over.

Pulling up to an abandoned house, Phillip sees a man standing beside a car.

"You got the money?"

"I got the money. You got the video?"

"Yeah, 'st right here." The man plays with the video in his hand. "Now toss the bag."

Fillip throws the bag at the man, but more in the air to see how he reacts.

The man, not thinking about feeling Fillip doing anything to him, reaches up to catch the money, but before he can even grab the money with a tight grip, Fillip takes out a gun and shoots him in the stomach.

The man falls on the ground, yelling, "You shot me, you bitch! I'll kill you and that hoe! I'll take your whole family away!"

"Nice words for a dead man crying on the ground like a little girl." Fillip walks up to him and points his gun.

"Wait, wait, you can't kill me. You not a killer. Don't get blood on your hands for someone like me."

"No, you're right, I can't kill you yet. Where did you get the video?"

"Like hell. I'm not telling you."

Fillip shoots the man again in the knee. "I see who you got it from. Do you need another bullet?"

"Okay, okay, I'll tell you if you don't kill me, you crazy fuck."

"Umm, okay, I won't kill you. It would leave a nasty flavor in my mouth."

"Okay, it was a young teen who gave it to me. He said he had a good video he was selling."

"Give me a name and where he is."

"Ya ya ya, he be on the curve of Sixteenth Street by the old toy store."

"Okay, you better not be lying."

"I'm not."

But before he can talk again, Fillip shoots the man four more times in the chest. In order to make it look like a robbery, Fillip left some money and drugs at the scene.

Walking away with a numb face, Fillip tells himself he's willing to do anything to see his baby girl happy. He can get over losing Alesha, but his daughter won't. She will suffer, and that's something he will not let happen. He'll do anything for her smile.

Fillip finds the boy's location and talks to him. "Hey, a friend of mine told me to ask you if you have any other copies of that video and did anyone else see it."

"Null, man. I was fucking a bitch in the woods when it happened, and you don't have to worry about her talking. I fucked her real good."

"You for sure? Don't make me come find you again."

"Ya, man, her mouth permanently closed, if you know what I mean."

Fillip looks at the boy beside him. "You don't need to be hanging with people like him. I advise you to leave before he get you into something you can't get out."

"Whatever, dude."

"Why you looked so nervous, dude?"

"He had a gun, you dumbass, and you sitting up here looking like *Blue's Clues*."

Fillip drives up the road, turns around, and drives back by the boy. On the way, he sticks a gun out the window and airs it out. The boy with the video gets shot in his chest and start choking on blood. The other boy gets shot in his arm and leg. He sees the other boy choking and just looks at him with a look of amazement. He crawls over to the boy and slowly puts his hands over his mouth. The more the boy kicks and cries, the bigger his smile grows till the boy has no energy left to fight. He hears the ambulance come and puts the boy on his side to make it look like he was trying to help the boy.

Earlier that day, but not too earlier, Alex is walking back and forth in his room, trying to itch an itch that couldn't be itched. He doesn't know what is wrong; he only knows he has to do something—and fast.

Then he gets a call from one of his friends who he smoked with. "Yo, dude, you trying to smoke something and maybe hit some girls up?"

Alex, who has a knife in his hands, gets a good thought, one that can fix his problems. "Yeah, the normal spot. I'll meet you there."

Later that day, Alex and his friend sit outside a store smoking and talking about a girl they wanna see till a man comes and talks to his friend.

Alex can tell the man has a gun and his friend is scared, but it excites him. After the man leaves, Alex's friend talks shit to him, but Alex still can't get over the feeling he was feeling, not till he hears loud shooting going off and feels a warm sting in his arm and leg. Alex looks over and sees his friend choking. He knows he won't get this opportunity again, so he takes it.

A few days later, Alesha decides that she wants to patch things up with her sister and move on with her life, even though her memories still remind her of the time she did and the pain. She'll let it go for the love she found and the new life she is building.

At Alice's house, Alesha knocks on the door. Alice goes and sees who it is. As soon as she sees Alesha's face, she closes it as fast as she can.

"Alice, I'm not here to fight or start anything. I'm trying to make things right."

"It's too late for that, don't you think, considering what you did?"

"Well, Alice, you're not too clean yourself. Who that baby daddy is? Yeah, I know your big secret."

Alice runs to the door. "You hush. You come to my house talking about peace and start saying shit like this? This ain't peace. You trying to destroy my life more." Alice lets Alesha in. "Why can't you just leave me alone?"

"Well, think about if I left you alone, you would have got fucked by the man till there was nothing left. Yes, I saved you and got sent away for it, but I'm not here to talk about the past."

Alice puts her head down. "So what you want?"

"I told you, I want to let all the hate go. I'm done fighting with you."

"So you not gonna say anything about the baby?"

"No, you have to deal with that. It's not like you knew y'all was related, even though he was way too young for you, but then again, your life was a living hell, so I don't blame you. Look, I say we live the best way we can. The world owes us that much, and if not, we take it, it's that simple. If you need anything, call me, and we can work out everything ourselves. You know how far I'll go for the people I care about, but don't do nothing illegal. I like my new life."

On the way in the house, Jason and Tyler see Alesha talking to Alice and walking out the door.

"Alice, why you talking to her?"

"Jason, who is she?"

"That's my sister and your aunt, Jason. By the way, you wouldn't be here if it wasn't for her, but I'm not getting into that right now. We putting the past behind us and coming together as a family."

"Okay, well, we're going to my room."

*****

A few days later, in another town over, a couple of robbers are on the run.

"Tom, slow down. Slow down, man, you're gone get us all killed driving like this. We been lost the fucking police. You'll just bring attention to us driving fast, and that will get us fucking caught. I told y'all this wasn't gone be easy. Shit got messy, so just suck it up and deal with it."

"Dammit! I got a family. It wasn't supposed to go down like this. Fuck you, Tom. Why you shot the man? You didn't have to shoot him," Jake expresses.

"I did what I had to do, that's just the way it is. Now we got the money, and that's the only thing that matters right now, so I apologize if things got a little messy."

Terry says, "Fuck it, I have a family too, so this shit is not right. If I'm gone, then who gone take care of my son? I had everything riding on this job, and your fuck-up almost got us all killed because ya'll didn't follow the plan."

"Now that's on you, Tom. Just because you have nothing, it doesn't mean we're the same."

Tom says, "Slow down," Terry."

Terry nearly wrecks.

"Shit, slow down! You're gone get us killed."

Terry repeats, "Fuck fuck fuck" while hitting the wheel. "I didn't sign up for this shit."

Jake speaks up. "No one signed up for this, but he sure did fuck it up though, ain't that right, Tom? Yeah, you just had to kill someone. Hell, to make matters worse, we still ain't get all the money, so somebody gone come up short, and it gone be you because this on your head."

Meanwhile, in the back, the robber named Kevin is frustrated. "It won't stop. I won't stop bleeding. Help me, somebody help!"

Blake says weakly, "I'm cold, I'm cold." He starts crying. "I don't want to die. I'm scared."

"Shit, I can't stop the bleeding."

Jake says, "He needs a hospital. He needs a fucking hospital. Shit, he's only sixteen."

Tom says angrily, "No, it's too hot at a hospital. We can't risk it."

Jake calls Tom's name. Tom says no. Jake calls Tom's name again, and Tom says no again.

"Dammit, Tom, he's dead. Tom, he's dead! And you know what? His blood is on your hands, so I hope you can deal with that, knowing your mistake caused all this."

Terry is driving faster and faster. "What we supposed to do now?" He is breathing hard and fast."

"We need to lose the body and find a way to destroy the car."

Terry continues panicking and shaking. "I can't go to jail. I can't go to jail. How it came to this?" Terry knows what he has to do, but can he do it? Can he take another life with his hands?"

Tom instructs, "Terry, get it to—"

Before Tom finishes his words, Kevin turns around and shoots him. As Terry turns around, *boom!* There is a loud noise, and everything goes black.

"Kevin, you fucker, where you at?" Terry is crawling from out the van breathing heavily. "No no no, it got to be here. That dirty two-timing pig took the money and ran!"

"Help me, I can't move! Hey, hey, you! Can you help me? I have a little girl and fiancée. I can't hear them anymore. I think they need a doctor."

"I can see you over there!" Alesha tries to scream as she cries and pleads for help, knowing somewhere in her heart that Bella and Fillip might already be dead, but she can only pray and hope they're not.

Terry touches his face and realizes that his mask is gone. In his mind, he knows there is no other choice. Terry comprehends what he has to do, but doesn't think he will be able to do the unthinkable. He walks over to lady who's crying and looks her in her eyes with a look of someone who knows there's no coming back from what he has started. Terry picks up an object and starts hitting the lady in the head till she no longer makes a sound. He then runs as fast as he can away from the scene.

Minutes later, a stranger whispers, "Shush, lower you voice."

Another stranger replies, "I know, I think he's gone."

"I think I hear some—oh my god, she still alive. We have to help her, call 911!"

One of the girls walks toward what seems to be a bag. As the stranger looks at the bag of money, she thinks to herself, *Should I take the money?*

The other stranger is on the phone with the police, talking fast.

"Ma'am, ma'am, slow down. I can't understand what you're saying. Can you start off by telling me your name?"

"Okay, okay, my name is Jessica."

The operator continues, "Okay, Jessica, tell me what is going on?"

"Yes, there was a crash. One man ran and another man attacked a lady and ran also."

"Okay, ma'am, is there anyone else there at the scene with you that can help you keep watch?"

"Yes, my friend is with me."

"Okay, somebody will be with you in a few minutes."

"They will be here soon. Hey, little scary pussy, the police coming soon, so act normal."

"Act normal? Jessica, we just fucked and killed a girl nearby. What if they find her?"

"Don't worry, they won't go all the way over there. Plus that bitch had it coming. You said you wanted revenge. You wasn't complaining when you was drilling her while choking her."

"God, can you talk lower? What if she hears you? Will you do something to her?"

"I don't harm innocent people, and I don't know her. That's why I called for help." Inside Jessica's head, she hears a voice full of anger, an anger that comes from abandonment and the need to belong. "Little one, little one, you did good. I can feel the power from that wonderful sacrifice. Her soul was black as night, filled with despair, and grow as we take what we want."

*****

Later that day at the hospital, Alesha wakes up to the worst news she could receive. Bella passed away, and due to the wreck, she might not be able to have kids.

When Fillip sees Alesha awake, he walks as fast as he can to her and starts crying. "Baby, I'm sorry. I'm sorry. I don't know what to do. She's gone. I'll do anything to get her back. Why they had to take her from me?"

The doctors rush in and pull Fillip up. "She needs her rest. I know you need her, but she needs rest right now. You have to be strong and get the people who did this."

The other doctor beside him corrects him. "The police are looking into everything, sir. You just sit down and be ready to help her recover."

Alice decides to go to the hospital to check on her sister and let the past go. Besides, she might need her help with something later on, plus, she knows too much. Alice gets a phone call from Beth.

"Hey, Alice, what are you doing?"

"I'm on the way to the hospital to check on my sister. She was in a hit-and-run."

"Oh, you and her talking now?"

"Yes, we talked it out. It's time to heal now."

"Well, okay, let me know if you need anything."

Alice and Fillip talk it out and get an understanding of each other. Fillip is trying to stay strong. Even though he lost his daughter, he still got to be there for the person he loves.

Alice decides to get on the phone and tell Beth what happened and that she's patching everything up with her sister.

Later on that day, the doctor tells them Alesha will be all right and that she just needs time to heal.

Walking in Alesha's room is Jasmine. As Alice hangs up the phone and turns around, she drops it in surprise of what she sees. "Oh great, I guess I'm dead since I'm seeing this dead crackhead."

"No, baby, you're not dead, and before y'all go crazy, I came to apologize, even if it's the smallest and only thing I can do."

"We must have died and gone to hell, Alesha, because I'm seeing a devil."

"I know y'all mad from what I put y'all through, but that is a little too harsh, Alice. Look, I'm not here to argue with y'all. I came to check on y'all and tell y'all something I thought y'all should know."

"What can you possibly tell us that will matter to us?"

"Y'all biological father was killed."

"What father? I'm confused."

"Alice, please!"

"She's right. What father is you talking about?"

"The man who came just to ask for money."

"Wait wait wait, I got enough shit on my plate. Do you not see me? How the fuck you alive?"

Jasmine explains everything to Alice and Alesha and decides to leave for now.

"That bitch dropped this on us and left. I see she is still crazy."

Days later at Alice's house, Jason and Tyler play the game. Jason can't help but feel the difference in Tyler. "Yo, dude, I know you been through a lot, but you been acting real different. I mean real, real different. Oh, what about that older girl you said you was fucking? What happened to her?"

"I wasn't fucking her. I fucked her. It was a one-time thing I don't even know her name."

"I'm surprised too."

"Jason, go grab me something to drink."

"You go get it yourself, dude. It's not like you new here. You been here more than me." When Jason said them words, a thought popped up in his head, but he brushed it off.

Walking toward the fridge, Tyler sees Alice and looks at her stomach poking out. He walks to her and puts his hand on her stomach.

Alice pushes his hand away. "Don't do that. What if Jason sees you?"

"He's playing the games. He didn't even want to get up and get me something to drink." Tyler looks at Alice for a couple more seconds.

Ding dong!

"That's probably my mom coming to pick me up."

Alice unlocks the door.

"Hey, Alice, how are you doing?"

"We are doing all right."

"I see your little baby growing."

"Yes, nice and healthy, at that I'm lucky."

"By the way, my husband has a friend who is a good guy. If you're interested in getting to know him, we can invite him over."

"Sure, I think that would be good."

"Oh, and he got a little boy. Will that be okay?"

"Yes, I don't mind that."

"Okay, well, you can come over tomorrow. Come on, Tyler. You got some cleaning to do. Your room looks a mess. I think I'm gone tell your dad not to get you that car he is thinking about getting you."

A day later at Fillip's house, Fillip and Alesha are getting ready to go to Bella's funeral.

"Baby, listen. Bella's momma gone be at the funeral, so please be patient, and don't let anything bother you. If she says anything, try to walk away."

"I know. I'm going to support you, plus I loved Bella too."

Later that day, Fillip's baby momma, Keira, asks Fillip if she can stay with him.

"Baby, I know y'all lost a daughter, but her staying here a little too much, do you think?"

"Alesha, she just lost her daughter. I just lost my daughter. Are you jealous right now?"

"I looked after her like my own daughter! How dare you say that! And I might not be able to have children. What about my feelings and pain?"

"I care about you. I'll do anything for you, so don't make Bella sad by being a bad person and not helping those in need. You the one I love. I'm not gonna let our hard work go to waste. Look at what we're building."

Keira listens to Fillip and Alesha talk things out. She loosens her clothes up and walks into Fillip and Alesha's room. "Oh, I'm sorry. With everything happening, I forgot you're in a relationship now. I'll leave."

"No, you're all right, just knock next time. What do you need?"

"I wanna taste Bella's favorite food. I was wondering if you could cook it for me."

"That's a good idea, Alesha. I think you'll like it too."

Keira looks at Alesha with a smirk.

At Beth's house Alice and Beth sit in the living room waiting for Ben to come with his friend.

"Beth, this is my friend Kevin. Kevin, this is my wife Beth and a close friend of ours, Alice."

About the Author

Thank y'all for taking an interest in my first book I'm just a young man from the county. I like things like gaming, art, a lot of music, etc. I'm trying to bring a little joy and excitement to the world. I don't focus on one genre. I love to mix emotions. So hop on the train with me, and let's see where it goes.